P9-CFU-917
Book #8
Slightley
damaged 5/23
Poor

Tree-House Comix Proudly Presents
DOG MAN
FETCH-22
WRITTEN AND ILLUSTRATED BY DAV PILKEY
AS GEORGE BEARD AND HAROLD HUTCHINS
WITH COLOR BY JOSE GARIBALDI
graphix
AN IMPRINT OF
SCHOLASTIC

FOR MY EDITOR AND FRIEND, KEN GEIST

The term "race car brain with bicycle brakes" on page 35 was coined by Dr. Edward M. Hallowell, M.D., co-author of *Delivered from Distraction: Getting the Most out of Life with Attention Deficit Disorder.*

Library of Congress Control Number 2019944440

978-1-338-32321-4 (POB)
978-1-338-32322-1 (Library)

10 9 8 7 6 5 4 3 2 1   19 20 21 22 23

Printed in China   62
First edition, December 2019

Edited by Ken Geist
Book design by Dav Pilkey and Phil Falco
Color by Jose Garibaldi
Color flatting by Aaron Polk
Publisher: David Saylor

CHAPTERS

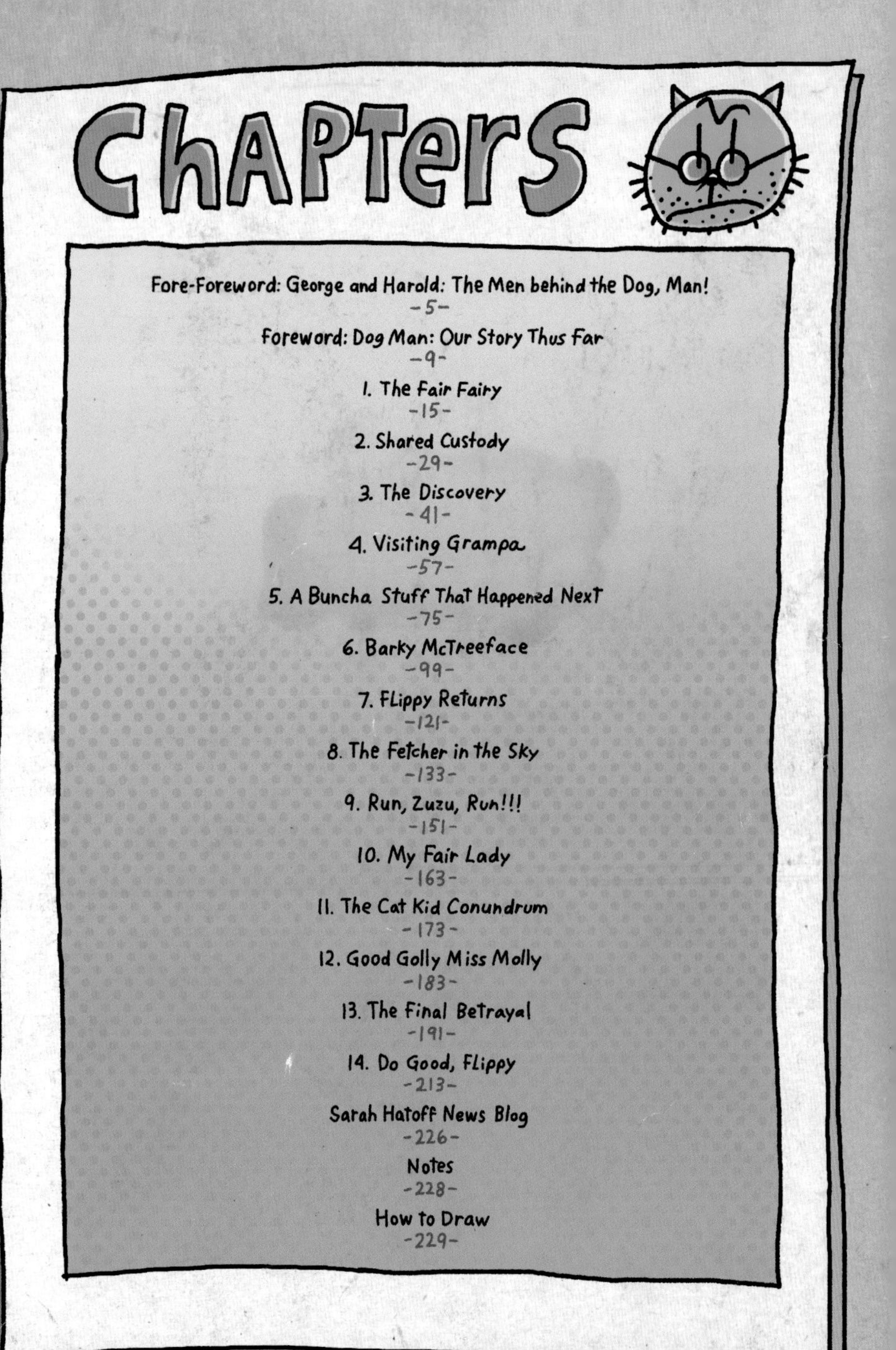

INTRO #1
George and Harold
The Men behind the Dog, Man!
Yo, SNOOPS!!! It's your old Buddies George and Harold!
'Sup?
We Just started 6th Grade a few months ago.
My, how Time Flies!
Now that we're GROWN-UPS, we've got some work to do!
So we're cleaning out our tree house.
TRASH
Yep! We're getting rid of all this KiD STUFF...
TRASH
Super Diaper Baby
... To make room for GROWN-UP STUFF!

"When I was a child, I spoke like a child...
Goodbye, Super Diaper Baby comics.
Super Diaper Baby
TRASH
...I thought like a child...
So long, Chubbs McSpiderbutt action figures and accessories.
...I reasoned like a child...
Farewell, homemade Pizza Box of Doom Playset.
DANGER: KEEP OUT!
TRASH

...But when I Grew up,
I put away childish things."
TRASH
PLOP!
TRASH
TRASH
WAAAAA

I Don't wanna be a Grown-up!!!

me neither!

Let's be Kids Forever!!!

Okay!!!

TRASH

And So...

POW!

Farewell, CHUBBS McSpiderbutt! You Shan't survive my Juice Box of woe!!!

Peeew Peeew

Not So Fast, Ambassador Babyhead!!!

Pow Pow Pow

Peeew Peeew Noooo

MWA-HA-HA-HA!

6TH GRADE! OH, YEAH!!!

6TH GRADE!!! Party Time!!!

While we ~~play with dolls~~ continue our pursuit of extreme Maturity, Please enjoy our Latest foray into Supa-Sophistication.

INTRO #2

DOG MAN

Our Story thus Far:

And Doggy—Your body is dying!!!
whine whine
ALL Hope is Lost!!!
No it Ain't!
Nurse Lady
Let's stitch the dog's head onto the cop's body!!!
Great idea, nurse lady!
And soon, an awesome new Hero was Born!!!
HOORAY FOR DOG MAN!!!
But then, things got complicated...

Petey the cat was busy Living a Life of wretchedness...

HAW HAW!

...When he accidentally created a Kitty clone.

CLONING MACHINE

START

DNA

Papa?

Petey tried to make his little clone become evil...

...but it was not to be.

KISS

Li'l Petey's Kindness melted his Papa's heart...

... and now they are a family.

During the week, Li'l Petey lives with his Papa in a secret laboratory.
They build awesome robots together.
But on the weekends, Li'l Petey lives with his OTHER family.
80-HD: The world's most Remarkable Robot Buddy.
Their House.
DOG MAN
FLIP FLOP FLIP FLOP FLIP FLOP FLIP FLOP
Together they play and make comics and stuff...
...but when help is needed, they transform into Superheroes!!!

Don't tell anybody, though. It's a secret!!!
WORST SECRET EVER!!!
I know! They just changed their costumes Right in front of us!!!
chief
Those guys talkin' smack over there are their friends.
SaraH: World's Best ReporTer.
ZUZU: World's bravesT Poodle.
CHieF: World's Chiefiest ChieF.
chieF
Together, they all fight to save the world!
Even Petey is Part of the Team!
I am Not!!!
chief

In our Last adventure, Petey was Reunited with his Long-Lost father.

It did not go well!

RENT 'N' MOVE

Petey's father stole all of their stuff...

...but he got busted by the cops.

Cat Jail

Now he's in the Slammer!

THAT'S NOT FAIR!!!

By George Beard and Harold Hutchins

Hey, fellas!!!
DOG Man
Hey, fellas!!!
The fair fairy's about to start!
Let's Go!!!
RiP!
FLip FLop FLip FLop

Hey, Kiddies...
FLIP FLOP FLIP FLOP FLIP
...It's time for every-body's favorite show:
THE FAIR FAIRY
Who's that fairy in the air...
...Who makes things completely fair?

She's the FAIR FAIRY! OH, YEAH!
Thank you, Downward Dog!
No Prob.
Before we begin today's show...
...I'd like to apologize for my little, uh...
..."bungle" on Last week's show.
Bungle?
Yes. I was under a lot of stress, and—

Dude, you went Totally BONKERS!
That's not true, Downward Dog!
And don't call me "dude." We've talked about that!
I WAS THERE, MAN! YOU FLIPPED OUT!!!
NOW, NOW— I've already apologized for—
HEY, GARY! Roll that Clip from LAST week!
NO!

Don't listen to him, Gary! He's CRAZY!
SHOW it! SHOW it! SHOW it!
DON'T YOU DARE!
The Fair Fairy
Film Clip: B-055
Episode 211
Air Date:
One Week Ago
Welcome back to our show, children!
Our next guests are Tina and Ramone.
Tina is upset because Ramone got TWO cookies...

...and She only got ONE!
Yeah! That's NOT Fair!
Well you've come to the Right Show!
Gimme that cookie, Ramone!
HEY!
SNAP
Here you go, Tina.
Now you each have one-and-a-half cookies!

That's not fair!!!
Why not?
She got ice cream yesterday - and I didn't get ANY!!!
munch munch
Hey, GARY! Do we have any ice cream backstage?
Here ya go, kid!
THAT'S NOT FAIR!
Why Not?
He got mint chocolate chip, but I only got Vanilla!!!

GARY!!! MORE ICE CREAM!!!
THAT'S NOT FAIR!!!
WHY NOT?
she got three scoops, but I only got two!
GARY!!!
THAT'S NOT FAIR!
WHY?

His ice cream has more chocolate chips Than mine!
Her spoon is bigger than mine!!!
My ice cream is all melty!!!
Mine is meltier than hers!!!
IT'S NOT FAIR!!!
ENOUGH!

GIMME THAT BOWL!
YOU GET NOTHING!
SMASH
And you GIMME YOUR BOWL!!!
NOTHING For You, Too!
CRASH
YOU BOTH GET NOTHING!!!
NOW IT'S FAIR!

NOW IT'S FAIR!
HA-HA-HA-HE-HE-HA-HA
The Fair Fairy
Film Clip: B-055
Episode 211
End of Clip
NOT APPROVED FOR REBROADCAST
See? I Told ya!
You were trippin,' dude!
WELL THAT WON'T HAPPEN AGAIN!!!

I'm much CALmer Today!
AND STOP CALLING ME "DUDE"!!!!!
Whatevs!
Now Let's welcome our first guests, Tim and Brenda.
Tim is angry because Brenda got two toys, and he only got one.
Yeah! IT's NOT FAiR!
NiNe Minutes LATer...

GIMME THAT TOY!
YOU GET NOTHING!
SMASH
NOW IT'S FAIR!
HA HA HA HE HE HA HA HE HA
Hey, Dog Man...
CRASH
Click
... was that show inappropriate?

CHAPTER 2
SHARED CUSTODY
By George Beard and Harold Hutchins

Soon...
Hey, fellas, it's almost five O'clock!
That means my Papa is gonna come over.
He's going to take me to his house for the week!
Remember our plan?
OK! Let's do it!!!

And so...
DOG Man
OH. Hey, Kid!
Hi, Papa!
DOG MAN
Are ya ready to go?
Yeah.
DOG Man
I just gotta get my backpack!
DOG Man
DOG Man
DOG Man

PLOOP
DOG MAN
KLUNK
KLUNK
WHAT the heck is IN THAT ThinG?
Umm...
HEY!
WHAT'S the BiG IDeA?

GET OUT OF THAT BACKPACK RIGHT NOW!
LOOK—WE HAD A DEAL!
You're supposed to live with ME during the week...
...And THOSE GUYS on the weekends, remember?
Yeah.

Well YA CAN'T bring them with you!!!
Rats!
NOW Let's GO!
Bye, fellas!
Hey, Papa...
...How come DOG Man and 80-HD Can't come and stay with us???

Because They CAN'T!!!
Why?
Look, I'm not trying to be mean...
...but Dog Man is a— he's just—
He'd lose his own HEAD if it wasn't sewn on!
And 80-HD is— he's just—
He's got a RACE CAR BRAIN with Bicycle BRAKES!

I just don't want those guys living in OUR house!!!
It's not fair!!!
Yeah, well, Life Ain't fair, kid. Get used to it!!!
Poopy-doopy-stoopy-floopy
AND STOP THAT WHINING!!!

Look, Kid. You're RIGHT! It isn't Fair!
YOU'VE got TWO families who love you...
...And there are Some Kittens out there who don't even have ONE famiLy!!!

You've got FOOD...
...a buncha BOOKS...
...TOYS, GAMES, ART SUPPLies...
...Some Kittens don't have ANY of those things!
HOW iS THAT FAiR??

You're right, Papa.
I Am?
Yeah. I'm sorry.
I was RIGHT about something?

I'll try to be more grateful.
I WAS RIGHT About SOMEThing!
Sweeeeet!!!

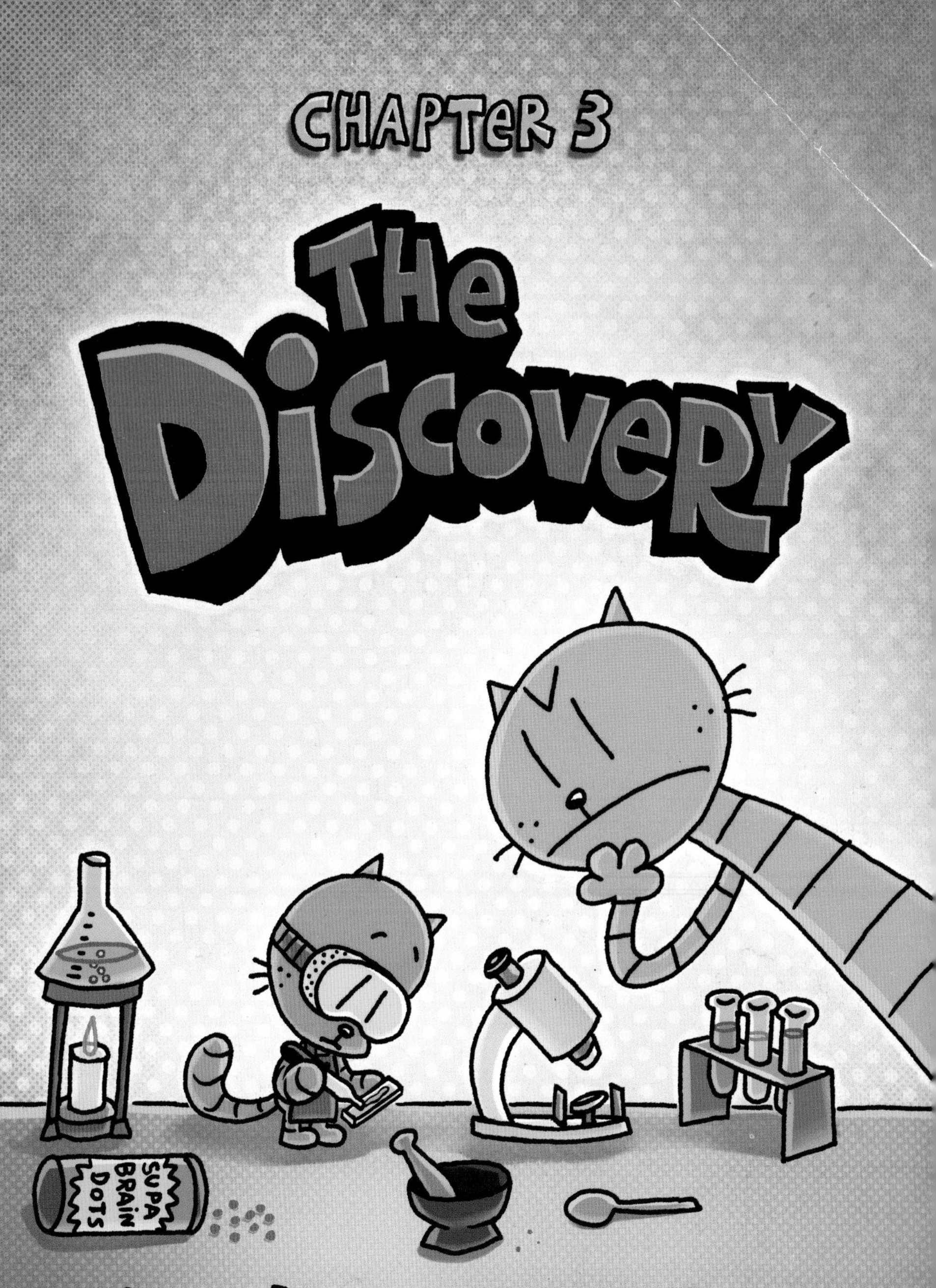

By George Beard and Harold Hutchins

The next day...
GASSY Behemoth Television
STUDIO A
Studio B
You wanted to see me, Larry?
MY NAME is SAM!
Whatever.
TAKE A CHAiR!!!
OK. I'll take this one.
HEY! Where DO YA Think you're Going?

YOU SAID I COULD T
SIT DOWN!
I'm still keeping the chair, Larry!
Look— we've had TONS of complaints about your show!
You're mean to the children, You're rude to the staff...
Flip
...You don't show up to work, You tell Lies CONSTANTLY...
FLIP FLIP

You steal people's lunches... You've got poor hygiene...
FLIP
...You're the WORST employee we've ever HAD!
Oh, Yeah? Well You're BALD!!!
GET OUT OF HERE! YOU'RE FIRED!
SLAM!
THAT'S NOT FAIR!
GASSY Behemoth Television

Meanwhile...
What'cha doing, kid?
SUPA BRAIN DOTS
I just made a discovery, Papa.
Supa Brain Dots contain a chemical called GR-2.
In high doses, it causes **SUPA ANGER!**
LOOK! This morning an **ANT** stole one of my Supa Brain Dots...
MWA-HA-HA
...and she started eating it.
NOM NOM

First she Got Psychokinetic Brain powers...
YAAAAAAAA!
... and she started moving things with her mind.
?
Then came the SUPA Anger!
I'll Get You!!
I drew these FLip-O-Ramas to show the progression!
the Progressive Stages of SUPA Anger in FLiP-O-RAMA™
Grrr!
INTRODUCING
FLiP

STEP 1.
First, Place your Left hand inside the dotted Lines marked "Left hand here." HoLd The book open FLAT!
STEP 2:
Grasp the right-hand Page with your Thumb and index finger (inside the dotted Lines marked "Right Thumb Here").
STEP 3:
Now QUICKLY fLip the right-hand page back and forth until the Picture appears to be Animated.
(For extra fun, try adding your own sound-effects!)
RAMA

While you are flipping, be sure you can see the image on page 49 **AND** the image on page 51.

If you flip quickly, the two pictures will start to look like **ONE ANIMATED** cartoon.

Stage 1
Anger
"Ant VS. Ant"
11:15 AM
Stage 2
AnGRier
"Ant VS. Beetle"
11:17 Am
Stage 3
Supa Anger
"Ant VS. Kid with
MagnifyinG Glass"
11:30 Am
Right
Thumb
here.

Sta
AnG
"Ant VS
11:15
Sta
AnG
"Ant VS
11:17
Sta
Supa
"Ant VS.
Magnify
GLASS"
11:30

OKay. So what?
FLIP
FLip
FLip
This proves that Flippy was innocent!
FLIPPY? Isn't he that bionic fish who tried to kill me?
Yeah, but it wasn't his fault.
The overdose of GR-2 Made him Supa Angry!
SUPA BRAIN DOTS
That's why They put him in fish Jail!
To: L.P.
your PAL, Flippy

But he's **CHANGED**, Papa. He's my friend now!
He's even in my comic club. See?
DINO-BUDDY
We make comics for each other every day!
DINO-BUDDY
THE END
BY FLIP
I don't want you getting involved with that crazy fish!!!
It's too Late, Papa. I already sent my findings to Sarah!
She's gonna do a news story about it!
SLAP

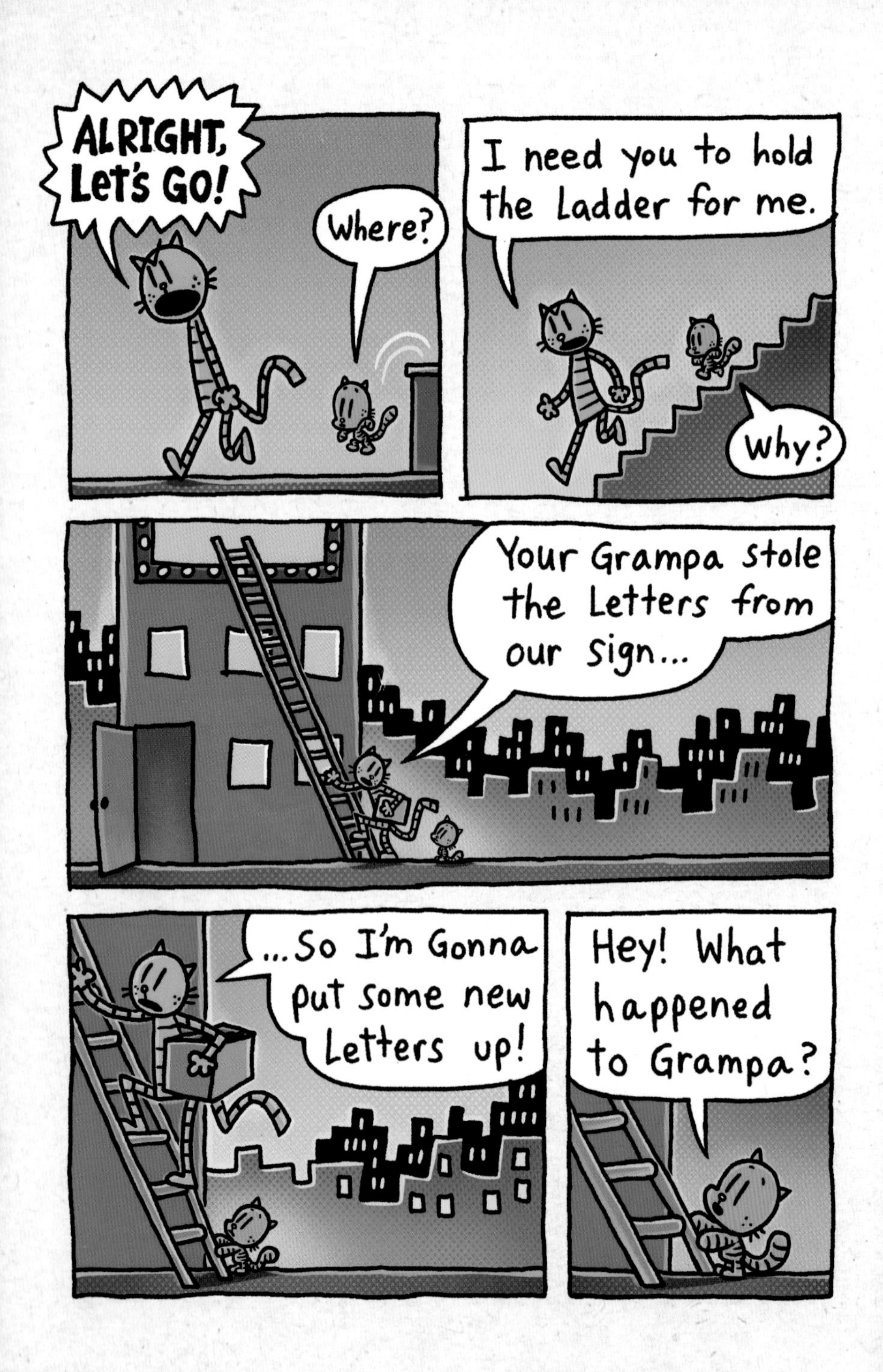
ALRIGHT, Let's GO!
Where?
I need you to hold the Ladder for me.
Why?
Your Grampa stole the Letters from our sign...
...So I'm Gonna put some new Letters up!
Hey! What happened to Grampa?

He got busted by the cops. He's in Cat Jail now!
Oh.
We should visit him!
ARE YOU CRAZY?
I Never want to see that guy AGAIN!
But he's your Papa!
Yeah! And he BETRAYED me!

PETEY &
But he's my Grampa!
HE BETRAYED YOU, TOO!
PETEY & SON
Trust me! That guy doesn't care about anybody but himself!
But Papa...
WE ARE NOT VISITING YOUR GRAMPA AND THAT IS FINAL!!!

By George Beard and Harold Hutchins

Hi! I'm Sarah Hatoff with Breaking News!
SARAH HATOFF
LIVE
A DRUG company has recalled all Jars of SuPa Brain Dots ...
TV
chief
But don't worry, folks!
chief
Right now, my most trusted officer...
chief
...is going to every store in the city...
chief
... and collecting all Jars of this dangerous drug!!!
chief

With Dog Man in charge, what could possibly go wrong?
chief
chief
chief
really?
chief
Meanwhile...
Roxy's Pharmacy
open
Roxy's Pharmacy

HEY!
Aren't you going to recycle those Jars at Least???
unscrew
unscrew
unscrew
SHAKA
SHAKA
SHAKE
BONK!
KLUNK

SHAKA
SHAKA
SHAKE
SUPA BRAIN DOTS
CLANK CLANK
KLUNK
SHAKA
SHAKA
SHAKE
SUPA BRAIN DOTS
ZOOM
SLAM
GET OUT OF HERE NOW!

Meanwhile...
It's so UNFAIR!!!
I can't believe Larry FIRED me!
I can!
He shoulda fired you a Looooong time ago, dude!
NOBODY ASKED YOU, DOWNWARD DOG!!!
whatevs.
I MUST Get my REVENGE!!!

I MUST find a way to make things FAIR!
Let me think...
...What I need is a MIRACLE!!!

Mirror, Mirror, by the tree...
...Who's the FAIREST? Is it ME?
Yeah!
WHO SAID THAT?
I did!

What the heck **IS** that thing?
I think it's a **TADPOLE**, Dude.
Hi!
Are you our Momma?
Look! There's TWO of Them!
I Think she's our Momma!
I Love you, Mom!
She's a nice Mommy!!!
I Love her, Too!
Now There's FOUR... Five... SEVEN... TEN...

Where are they all coming from?
Hello, Mommy!
What's up, Mom?
Hi, Mom!!!
I think they're hatching Right Now!
Why are they all calling me "Mom"?
Dude, it's called IMPRINTING! Look it up!!!
Eighteen--- nineteen--- twenty---
Hiya, Mommy!
She's the best mommy I ever had!
We Love You, Mom!
Mom! Look at Me!!!
She's so Awesome!!!
She's so Pretty!

---Twenty-one---
twenty-Two!!!
sniff
sniff
WAAAAAAA!!!
Why are you crying, Dude?
IT'S NOT FAIR!!!
ALL I ASKed for was A MIRACLe...
sniff
sniff
...but instead I got Twenty-Two baby tadpoles who think I'm their MOM!
AND STOP CALLING Me "DUDE"!!!

Meanwhile...
CAT Jail
I can't believe You talked me into visitinG Your Grampa!!!
He's just going to betray us AgAin!
Maybe he will, Maybe he won't!
But don't You think we should give him another chance?
NO, I DON'T!

You can't just Go Around TRUSTING EVERYBODY!!!
I know, Papa.
Some people are hard to love.
That just means ya gotta try harder!!!
Hey, Papa! Guess what?
What?
You're EASY to love!
Yeah, I know!

And so...
Cat Jail
Oh, Gramps!!!
WHAT?!!?
HEY!!!
What's Going on?
Are you Concocting Some Sort of **Sleep GAS** or something?

NO.
How to CONCOCT Some Sort of SLEEP GAS OR Somethin
SLEEP PILLS
SLEEPY-Head Tea
SLEEP GAS FORMULA
Oh, Good! That's a relief!!!
Well, come with me! You've got two visitors!!!
I KNEW they'd come!
HanG on a second!

Drip
Drip
Bubba
Bubba
Bubba
Squee
squee
FFFFFFFFFFFFFFFFFF
FFFFFFFFFFFFFFF
FFFFFFFFFFFF
Tie
Tie
ALRIGHT! Let's Go see those visitors!!!

Hi, GUYS!
VISITING ROOM
I've missed you so much, son!
Yeah, RIGHT!
And I missed you most of all, Li'L Ralphie!
Li'L Petey!
Yeah! Li'L PETEY! That's what I SAID!
Look! I brought you a present!
Thanks, Grampa!
And I even brought something for ME!

A Pin...
...and a gas mask!
NO-WAIT!
POP
Don't worry— it's just a harmless Sleep Gas.
By the time you WAKE up, I'll be FREE!

By George Beard 'n' Harold Hutchins

Welcome back to our news show!
chief
And look who's here! It's DOG MAN!
chief
He just finished collecting all of the SUPA BRAIN DOTS in the city!!!
chief
TV
Now nobody else will develop Psychokinetic Brain Powers...
chief
...OR become Supa AnGry!
chief

See? I TOLD ya nothing would go wrong!!!
chief
Shake a paw, DOG Man!!!
chief
chief
chief
chief
HEY!!!
TV
The WAGON is ROLLING AWAY!

chief
Get it, DOG MAN!
POW

PLIP Plip PLIP PLop PLIP PLOP PLippity PLOP PLop PLIP PLOP

Meanwhile...
cat Jail
Alrighty, then...
...The sleeping gas in the room has dissipated.
Now it's time for Phase 2 of my evil plan!
SSSSSSSHHHHHHH
SUPA SHAVE FOAM
SKRITCH SKRITCH

SKRITCH
SKRITCH
TWING
GLUE

SUPER-BINDING GLUE
PERMANENT MARKER
SQUEAK
SQUEAK
SQUEAK
SQUEAK
SQUEAK
SQUEAK
PERMANENT MARKER
ORANGE Juice
ORANGE Juice
POP!

Glug Glug Glug
ORAnge Juice
SUPA-BONDING GLUE
SQUIRCH
And now for the finishing touch!!!

Perfection!
But WAit!
POP
Orange Juice
PeeeeL
ORANge Juice
100% Juice
Okay, SLeepyhead! It's time to go!!!

OH, GUARD!
Yes, Petey?
My Dad just fell asleep!
Oh, dear! I'd better get him into bed!
CAT JAIL
And so...

Meanwhile...
What's happening to us???
My brain feels weird.
Mine too!!!
It's almost as if we've all developed psycho-Kinetic brain powers Somehow!!!
Yeah!
But how could such a thing have happened?
Beats me!
HEY!

Mommy! Where are you going???
I Ain't Your mommy, You little weirdos!!!
MOMMY!!!
Hey, MA!
COME BACK, MOMMA!
MOM!
Don't LeAVE US!!!

MMF MMBFMFF MUH, MOOF!!!
What?
MMF MMBFMFF MUH, MOOF!!!
You Shouldn't talk with your mouth full!
LOOK BEHIND YOU, DUDE!!!

Stay with us, Mom!
Mommy! Don't Go!
We Love You, Mom!
How did those UGLY things Learn to FLY?
Dude— maybe you shouldn't antagonize them!
STAY AWAY FROM ME, YOU SLIMY GREEN GOONIES!!!

I'm OUTTA HERE!
MOMMA! COME BACK!!!
What Should we do?
I've Got an idea!!!

RUSTLE RUSTLE
C-C-CRACK
GRRRRROAN
C'mon, everybody! Let's all work ToGether!!!

RRRRR
KRACKASMOOSH!
STOMP STOMP
FLIP-O-TRAUMA
Left hand here.

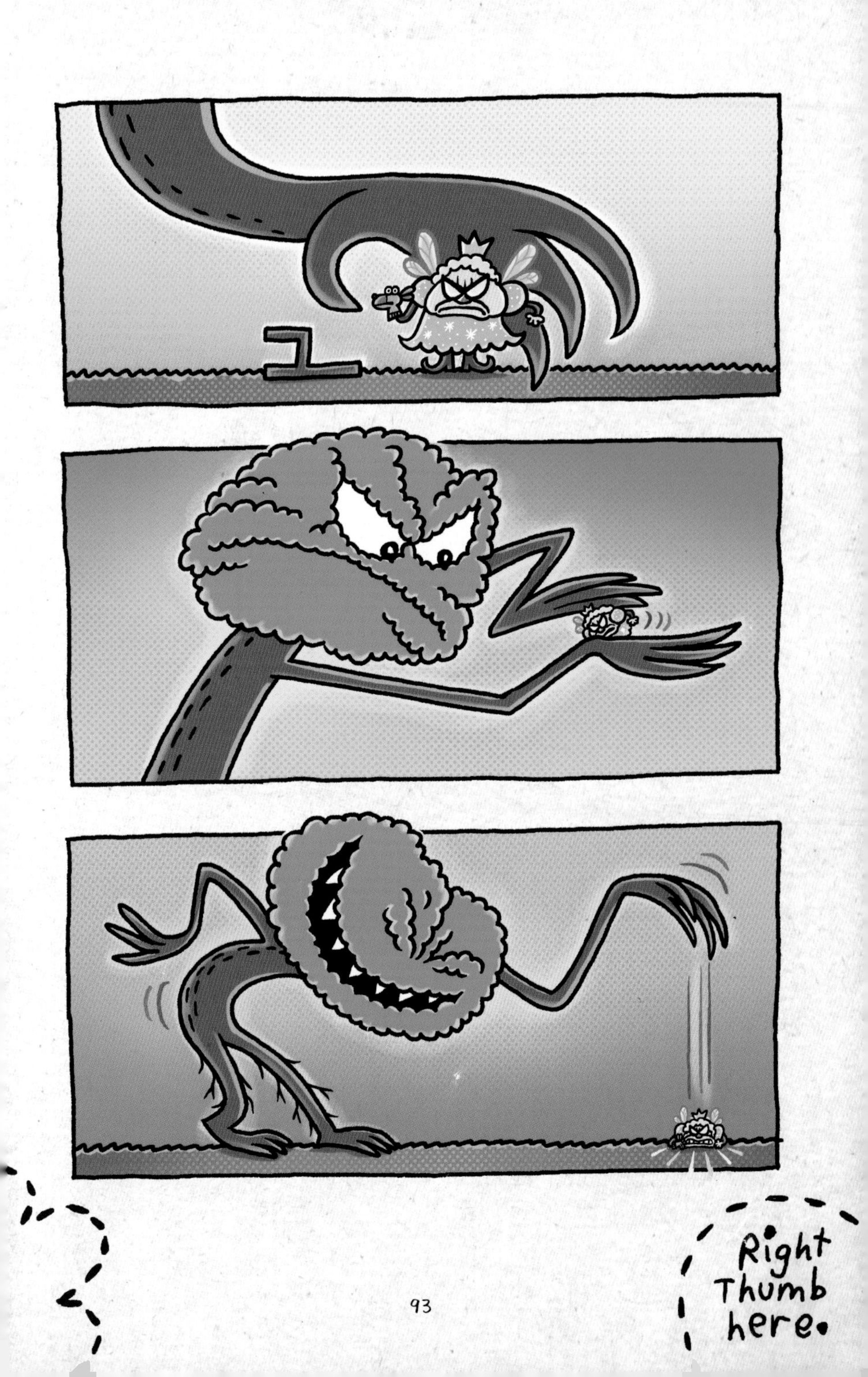
Right
Thumb
here.

STOP!
How did this TREE come to LIFE???
We're controlling it with our minds!
Yeah! We're SUPA Angry!
And we're not gonna let you leave us AGAIN!!!!!!!
Now, Now-Wait Just a minute!
Maybe we can all work something out!

What are you doinG, Dude?
Shhh! Don't you see? Those powerful little tadpoles...
...And this GiGantic MONSTER TREE...
...Are Just what I need to make EverythinG FAIR!
Oh.
Now PUT ME DOWN...
...and let's be a FAMILY!!!

Good! Now all we need is a name for this Tree Monster!
We must find a name that suggests UNLIMITED POWER...
...UNSTOPPABLE EVIL...
...AND ULTIMATE DESTRUCTION!!!
A name that will strike terror into the hearts of ALL!
I'VE GOT IT!

CHAPTER 6
BARKY McTREEFACE

We Are NOT Calling him "Barky McTreeface"!
Aw, come on, dude! That's a COOL Name!
THAT'S The DUMBEST NAME I ever HEARD!
Well I Like it.
So do I!!!
We LOVE Barky McTreeface!!!!!
Hey, Let's make up a Song about him!
Yeah!
OK!
Good idea!
YOU BETTER NOT!

Barky McTreeface was an eviL, Rotten BLoke...
STop That!
...He was rough and mean, and his face was Green...
... with Two arms made out of oak.
CUT that OUT!!!
Barky McTreeface...
...Was So Nasty, Rude, and tough.
THAT'S ENOUGH!

He was bad, it's True, but the tadpoles Knew...
...how he came to Life and stuff!
There must've been enchantment in...
... those Tadpoles from that swamp.
For when they Zapped him with their brains...
... he began to roar and stomp!
BOMP!

Down to the city...
... causing cataclysmic crime...

Punching here and there...
... Smashing everywhere...
... Now it's FLIP-O-RAMA Time!
DO IT!!!
Left hand here.

Right
Thumb
here.

Flippity Flip-Flip
Slappity-slap.
Look at Barky Punch!
Flippity Flip-Flip
Kickety-Kick.
He'll eat ya up for Lunch!

Haw Haw Haw! Look at that DESTRUCTION!
Now things Are becoming FAIR!
Wait a minute— How does THIS Make things Fair?
I Just Lost my JOB! I Lost EVERYTHING!
Yeah. So?
So now I'm taking EVERYTHING Away from EVERYONE else!

You See? Everyone Gets NOTHiNG!
Oh.
DO YOU HEAR Me? YOU GET NOTHING!!
NOW it's FAiR!
But wait, Mommy. There are still some buildings over there!
And some trucks and cars over there!!!
Well I can fix that!!!

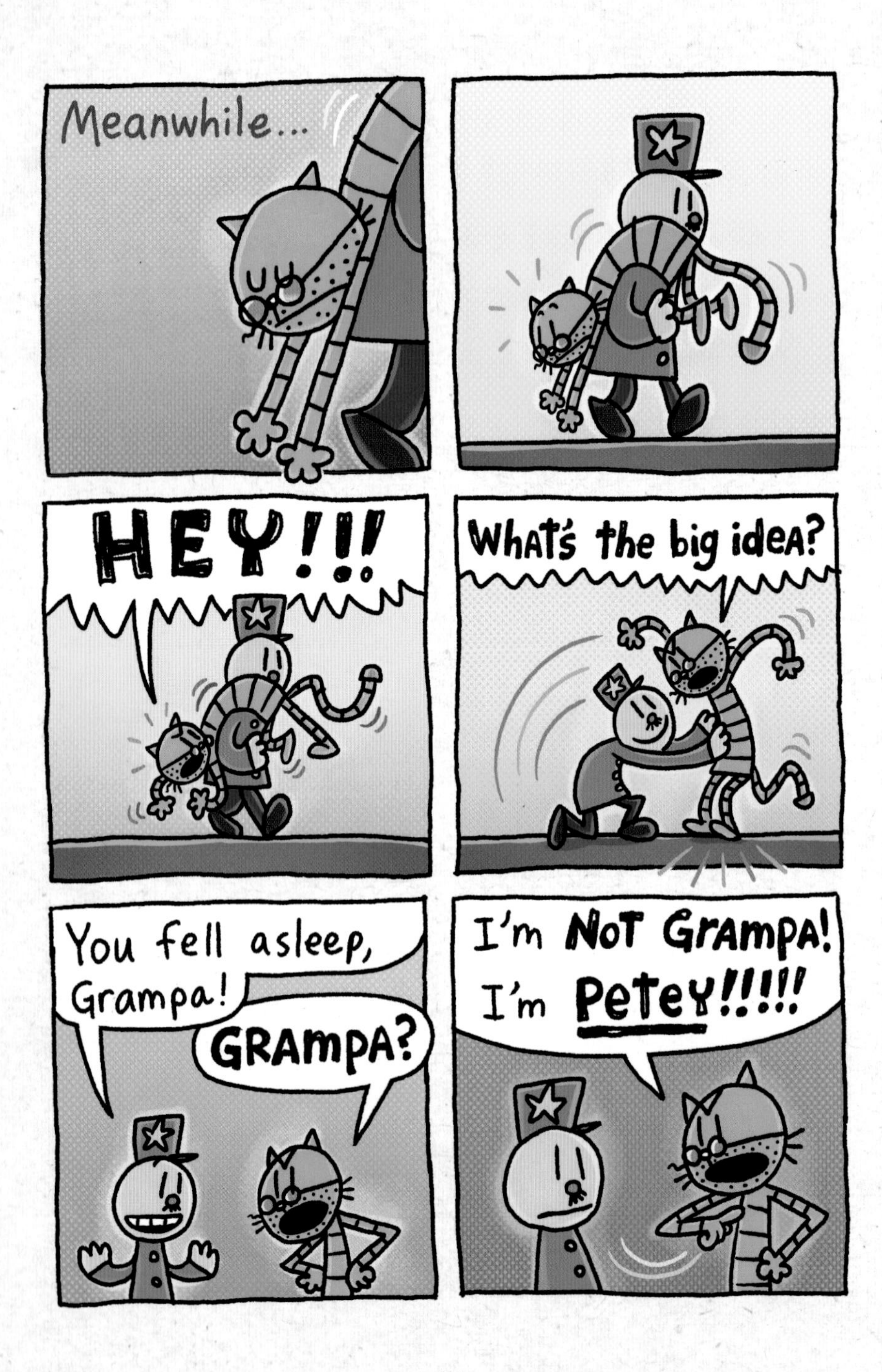
Meanwhile...
HEY!!!
What's the big idea?
You fell asleep, Grampa!
GRAMPA?
I'm NOT GRAMPA! I'm PETEY!!!!!

Ha! Silly Grampa!!
NO!
NO!
What's wrong, Grampa?
I'm NOT GRAMPA! These Aren't My GLASSES!!!

Yeah, but what about your taiL and whiskers???
That's just GLUE and MARKERS and stuff!!!
Sorry, Grampa! I'm not falling for your tricks AGain!
WAit A Minute—I've Gotta find my SON!

Oh, don't worry about him...
...Petey Left here about an hour aGo.
He had your little Grandson with him!
LOOK-You've got to Listen to Me!
THAT KiD is iN TeRRiBLe DANGER! LeT Me OUT OF HeRe NOW!!!

Okay, Grampa. Whatever you say!
The exit is through that door!
Wait! This is just an ordinary JaiL cell!!!
SLAM
HEY!

I fooled YOU This time, Grampa!!!!
LET ME OUT!!
I can't Believe I Got tricked AGAIN!
I'm really Losing my touch, man!!!
How could things Get any WORSE?
Hiya, roommate!!!
J

Meanwhile...
199
Ken's
KARAoke Club
Trash
Ken's
Ke club
Trash
YAWN!
Trash
Hey!

STOP
PETEY
&
SON
Hi, Grampa!

I'm NOT Grampa! I'm PETEY!!!
No you're not!!!!
Yes I Am!!!
No you're not!!!!
YES I AM!!!
No you're not!!!
YES I AM!!!
No You're not!!!
YES I AM!
No y
Not!
YES I AM!

Okay.
Hey, I'm Hungry!
Well go cook Some food then, ya freeloader!
What do I look like? Your SERVANT?
My Papa always cooks for me.
You DID say you were my Papa, didn't you?
SLAP!
And So...

Later...
PeTeY & SON
Hey, Papa!
What Now?
More Popcorn, please.
I'm NOT MAKinG ANY MORE POPCORN!
But my Papa Always makes more popcorn!
You DID say you were my Papa, didn't you?
THAT KiD IS DRIViNG Me CRAZY!
Pop Pop Pop
Pop Pop Pop
Pop Pop Pop

CHAPTER 7
FLIPPY RETURNS

Meanwhile...
FISH JAIL
Haw Haw Haw Haw!
MY eviL PLan is WORKinG!!!!!!!
Soon I shall take over the WorLd!!!
But first, I must destroy that Robo-cat!
HAW HAW HAW
The End.
MY STORY by FLIPPY
HAW HAW HAW

What happened next, Flippy?
CAT KID'S COMIC CLUB
Well, Let's turn the page and find out!!!
FLIP
Suddenly...
CRASH!
The End.
MY STORY
by FLIPPY
...The Robo-cat was in my Grasp!!!
Suddenly...
CRASH
...The Robo-cat was in my grasp!

But just as I was about to destroy my enemy...
...I met a little Kitten.
Hi!
He gave me a comic Book.
My Friend Flippy
He'd made it just for me.
My Friend Flippy
Nobody had ever been so kind to me before.
And as I read my comic with my new friend...
The end
My Friend Flippy

Something changed inside me...
The End
My Friend Flippy
...And all of my supa evil powers melted away.
I might not be a Tough guy anymore...
...but I am Living proof...
...that Love and Kindness...
...are the greatest powers of all.

The end.
The End.
Hooray!
Awesome!
Sweeet!
CAT KID'S COMIC CLUB
MY STORY by FLIPPY
YAY!
Bravo!!!
Thanks, everyone!!!
But then...
Hey, Flippy! the Mayor's on the phone!
MY STORY by FLIPPY
Hello?
Pack your bags, Flippy! You're a **Free Fish!**
I am?
Yep! Li'l Petey's Research Proved you were innocent!!!
M

I'm Free!
Congratulations, FLIPPY!!!
Let's Go Fill out the Paperwork...
...And Soon, all your problems will be over!
We interrupt this chapter with a tragic update:
chief
BREAKING NEWS
A Giant tree is attacking the city...
POW!
LIVE
...And it looks like it's being controlled by...
chief
LIVE

...Twenty-Two tiny TAdpoles!!!
LIVE
They all have Psychokinetic Powers...
LIVE
...And they all seem SUPA ANGRY!
LIVE
Gee – I wonder how THAT HAPPENED!
chief
LIVE
Well, uh, he was–
chief
LIVE
And DON'T BLame DOG Man! It WAS Your Fault, too!!!
chief
LIVE

...Well, uh...
...MISTAKES WERE MADE!!!
chief
LIVE
But don't worry, Folks! I've put Dog Man in charge...
...of fetching those twenty-Two tiny Tadpoles!!!
LIVE
Once he fetches them...
...we'll get them the help they need!
chief
LIVE

Who wants to Fetch the TAdpoles?
LIVE
Who's a good fetcher???
LIVE
Is it You? Is Dog Man a GOOD Fetcher?
LIVE
Who's Gonna fetch 'em? Who's a Good fetcher boy????
LIVE
READY???
LIVE
GO Fetch 'em!!!
ZOOM
LIVE

See? With DOG Man in charge...
...What could... uh, Possibly...
chief
LIVE
...g- go wrong?
YOU BETTER GO HELP him!
LIVE
Well, uh— Okay...
...But who's gonna Help me?
LIVE

LIVE
LIVE
Well, Zuzu, I guess it's up to us!!!
LIVE
Let's Go SAVE The World Again!
LIVE
Oh, boy, this is Gonna be GREAT!!!
LIVE

Tree-House Comix Proudly Presents
CHAPTER 8
The Fetcher in the Sky

Meanwhile...
Cat Jail
I'm so glad we're roommates, Grampa!
I'm NOT GRAMPA! I Already told ya, like, A MILLION TIMES!
I Know. And I believe you, Grampa!
Beep!

But then...
We interrupt this tenderhearted moment with Breaking News:
chief
Dog Man and Chief are heading to town...
...to stop the evil tree that is ATTACKING the city!
Evil Tree? Attacking the city?
This looks like a job for COMMANDER CUPCAKE!!!
J

Huff Puff Huff
Huff
Puff
Puff

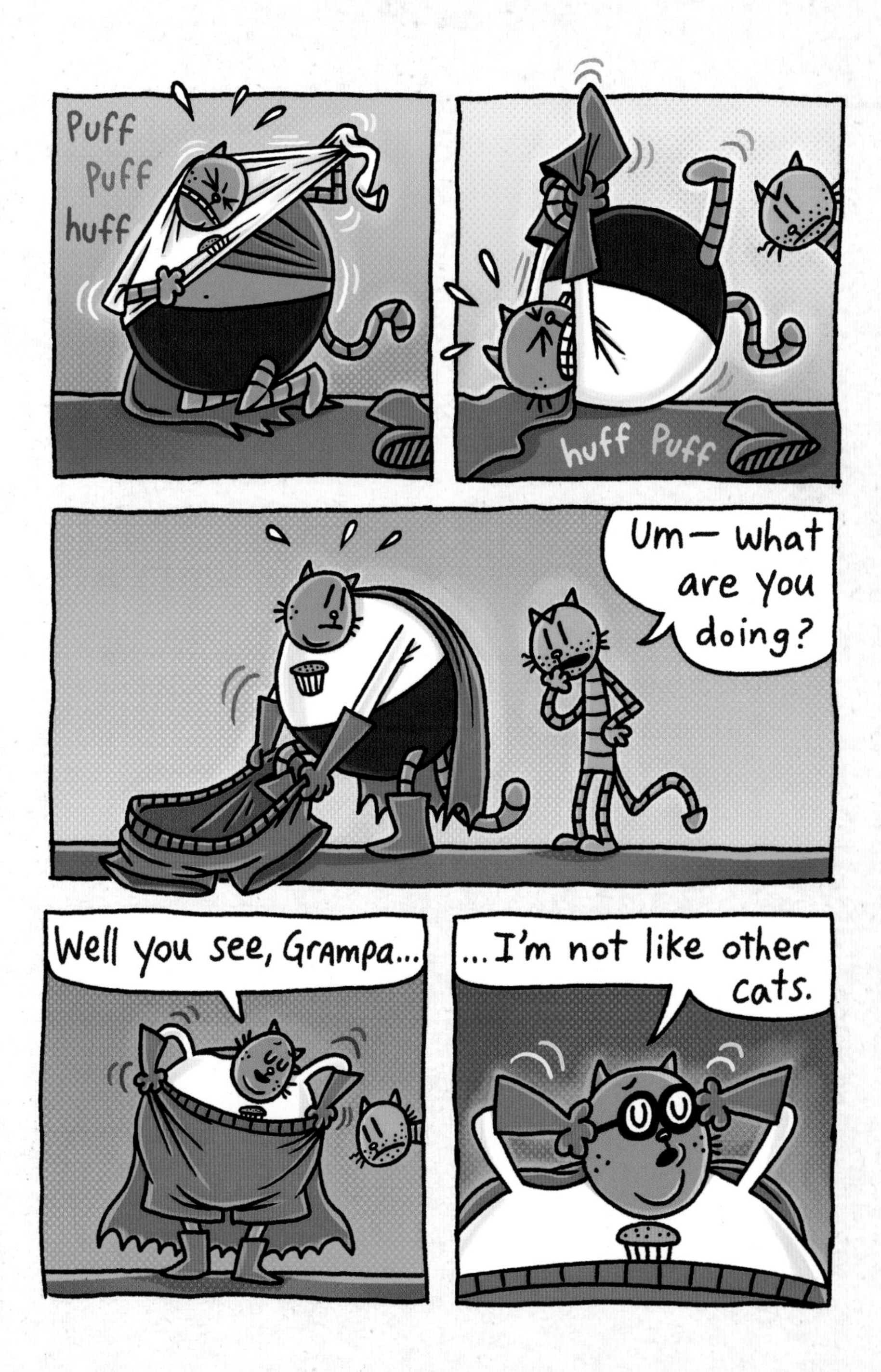
Puff
Puff
huff
huff Puff
Um— what are you doing?
Well you see, Grampa...
...I'm not like other cats.

You see...
...I fight for Frosting!!!
...I Stand for Sprinkles...

...And I champion the cause of carbohydrates!
Amen!
NOBODY CARES!!!

But--- But I'm Commander cupcake!
Well That's Just GREAT!
I was just thinking: what we REALLy NEED Right Now...
... is A Guy in a Cape whose ONLY Superpower is that he eats a lot of CUPCAKES!!!
I also eat sprinkles!
THAT'S NOT HELPFUL!!!

We're Stuck in here without A Key!!!
Psst! We don't need a key, Grampa!
We shall escape through my Cupcake Corridor!
ANG in HERE!!!
Watch this!
BONK!
HANG IN THERE!!!
HANG IN

HANG IN
YOU HAD AN ESCAPE TUNNEL THIS WHOLE TIME...
...AND YOU DIDN'T TELL ME??
You didn't ask!

Meanwhile...
chief
As Dog Man and his friends got closer to the scene of the crime...
chief
NETS
... they Grabbed some weapons...
chief
... and prepared for an epic Battle!!!

chief
It's time to give up, Fair Fairy!!!
chief
NEVER!!! You DO-GOODERS Can't stop my SUPA-ANGRY PSYCHOKINETIC TADPOLES!
STOP The TADpoles, DOG Man!!!
STOP The Dog Man, Tadpoles!!!
chief

And so...
SWISH

C'mon, Chief! Let's Get, those tadpoles!
RiGht!!!
chief
But then...
What's happening to my arms???
It's those TAdPoles! They're Zapping us with their Brains!!!
chief
...AND WE CAN'T CONTROL OUR ARMS ANYMORE!
chief
FLiP Like There's NO TOMORROW!!!
Left hand here.

Right
Thumb
here.

And so...
HEY!!!
Zip
DUDE! That Poodle is Getting away!!!
Aw, Let her go!
She's just a tiny poodle.
What could one tiny Poodle Possibly do?

CHAPTER 9
RUN, ZUZU, RUN!!!

Petey
&
son

You did, too!!!
I DiD NOT!
Oh, hi, Zuzu!
Screech
BARK BARK BARK!!!
What's that you say? DoG Man's in trouble?
RUFF RUFF BARK BARK BARK!
Sarah and Chief, too?

BARK BARK GRRR OWoooooooooo!
Unspeakable evil? Mindless chaos???
Unlimited Supa Powers with no moral compass?
This looks like a job for the SUPA BUDDIES!
C'mon, Zuzu!
slide

80-HD, Don't FAIL Me NOW!
Petey & Son
ZOOOOOOM

HEY!!!
Petey & Son
Unspeakable evil, eh???
Unlimited Supa Powers?
No moral compass?
Petey & Son

Meanwhile...
Well, here we are at Last, Grampa...
...MY Cupcake Command Center™.
Let's check the cupcake computer!
COMPYUDUH.
CUPCAKES
Yum
Eat it.

Click-clack-clickity clack-Beep-Boop...
COMPYUDUH.
cupcakes
Sprinkles
Yum
Eat it.
HeY! That's not a real keyboard!
It's just a Pizza box with stuff drawn on it!!!
...And ya spelled "Computer" wrong!!!
COMPYUDUH.
cupcakes
Yum
Eat it.
Look, We need to Get out of Here!!!
TO THE CUPCAKEMOBILE!

Behold: The Latest in Cupcake TechnoLogy!!!
I just need to GLue on the last PaPer PLate...
... I mean "TiRe"!
PBBBBBBT
Uh-oh...

Look, we haven't Got time for this!
I've gotta go and save my SON!!!
But you haven't seen the cupcake cabana yet...
...or the cupcake croquet court...
...or the–
I JUST WANNA SEE The CUPCAKE EXIT!!!

Well Why didn't You Say So???
SLAP
Hey!
I think your back got Stuck on my hand Somehow!!!
OH, well — come on, Grampa!

ATOMIC CUPCAKE POWERS ACTIVATE.
PBBBBBT!
CUPcake Exit
PBBBBBBBBT!!!
PBBPBBBBPBBBBT
cupcake entrance

CHAPTER 10
MY FAIR LADY

Hello again, folks! I'm Sarah Hatoff Reporting from...
.. a floating net.
We've all been captured by twenty-two Supa-angry psychokinetic tadpoles...
..And they're holding us in the sky with their Brain Powers.
How will we ever get out of this mess???

SNIP
SNIP
SNIP
chief
BUMP BINK BOMP
Gee, that was a lot easier than I thought it would be!!!
chief
And Look, Flippy the bionic Butterfly fish...
...has joined our fight for GOOD!

But there's only four of us!!!
And twenty-five of us!!!
How will we ever get out of this mess?
Never fear, Sarah!!!
ZIP
IT'S SUPA BUDDY TIME!
COSTUMES

Meanwhile...
PBBBPBBBPBBBBT!!!
HEY, GRAMPA!
Coco's
Cupcakes
Yum!
Open 24 Hrs.
Yum!
HoT coffee
Our prayers have been answered!!!
...WAIT— NO WAY!!!
Coco's
Cupcakes
LOOK!
Coco's
Cupcakes
Yum!
Open 24 Hrs.
Yum!
HoT coffee

COCO'S CUPCAKES
We must eat that Gigantic cupcake!
It's not REAL, ya know!
Only then can we Save the world!!!
It's Just a SIGN!!!
ALmost there...
COCO'S CUPCAKES

Meanwhile...
HUFF PUFF HUFF
At Last I've found You!
Who the heck are YOU?
Allow me to introduce myself!
I'm your NEW Partner in Crime!
PARTNER? What do I need a Partner for?
Can't You see I'm Just about to Defeat the SUPA Buddies?

Indeed she was Right. The Supa Buddies and their friends...
chief
...had Given their all...
chief
...and had put up a valiant Fight.
(Good Vibes)
But they were outnumbered...
CRASH!

... outmatched...
PUNT
... and out of time!
YOINK
One by one, our heroes were captured...
CHIEF
...And the powers of evil grew stronger and stronger.
BARK
BARK
BARK
Ruff
Ruff
Ruff
Look at me!!!
I'm FLYING, BABY!

I'm the Queen of the WORLD!
But, Mommy...
...We still haven't captured Cat Kid!
He must be hiding somewhere, Dude!
Aw, don't worry about him!
What could one tiny Kitten possibly do?

CHAPTER 11
The Cat Kid Conundrum

Meanwhile...
... in the quiet of night...
... in the stillness of twilight...
... a silent sentinel sneaks in the shadows.
swiftly...
...unsuspecting...
...He shings his claws.
SHING

Ready to slice.
And in this perfect moment...
...When a swipe from his sharpened sabers...
...Promises sweet salvation...
...he stops.
SHING

HEY!
I didn't see ya back there.
You could have clobbered me!
I know.
You could have sliced us all into sushi.
I know.
You could have saved all of your friends.
I know.
But you didn't.

Why?
I can't hurt you guys.
You're just little kids.

What's your name?
Molly.
Oh. I'm Li'l Petey.
Hey, guess what? I have a comic club!
You do?
Yeah. You can join if you want to.
But I never made a comic before.
It's okay.
I can show ya how. It's FUN!!!

You'll teach me?
Of course.
That's what friends do. They help each other.
As the two friends talked and laughed, Something started to change in Molly...
Ha Ha Ha
Ha Ha Ha
... and soon, her Supa Anger began melting away.
WHAT'S GOING ON HERE?!!?

Mommy, this is Li'l Petey!
He's my FRIEND!
NO HE'S NOT!!! He's YOUR ENEMY!
But, Mommy, I think–
YOU'RE NOT SUPPOSED TO THINK!!
YOU'RE SUPPOSED TO OBEY!

Here! Take this Kitten!!!
But, Mommy!!!
CReeAK
SNAP
Mommy, WAit!!!
Alright, children— it's time to destroy the Supa Buddies and their friends!!!

That's Right, Kiddies! Zap them with your SUPA-Angry Powers!!!
Mommy, NO!!!
See? Nobody else has a problem with following orders!!!
Now Get down there with all of the others...
...AND DO AS YOU'RE TOLD!

CHAPTER 12
Good Golly
Miss Molly

It is easy to join with the crowd...
...and even easier to spread anger and hate.
But it takes courage to stand alone.
And kindness often takes the most courage of all.

Molly could not move the mighty tree all by herself...
CHIEF
... but she could move a branch...
C-C-CREAK!
... and that was all she needed.

C'mon, gang! I've got an idea!!!
They're Getting Away!!!
Aw, Let 'em Go!
What could one tiny tadpole and one tiny Kitten and one tiny poodle Possibly do?
DUDE— seriously?

DOG Man
Hey, what's up, 'Puter?
'Sup?
Supa 'puter
We need your help, brah!
'K

We need to create an ANTIDOTE to Supa Brain DoTS.
No prob. I'll download the components...
...then calculate a recipe for our concoction using everyday ingredients.
Sweeet!
C'mon, gang! Let's go find some everyday ingredients!!!
And soon...
MINI MARSH-MALLOWS
Ok, what next?

...now add two teaspoons of ketchup...
TOMATO KETCHUP
...and a dash of paprika...
SHaka
Shaka
Shake
Paprika
Lastly, pour the mixture into my subcritical fission reactor.
One Nuclear Trans-mutation Later...
DinG
Supa 'puter

And So...
OKay, We're all ready!
Does everybody understand the plan?
Yeps!
Bark! Bark!
OKay! Good Luck!
Let's Go!!!
DOG Man

CHAPTER 13
THE FINAL BETRAYAL

Soon...
Hi, Papa!
Where have YOU been?
Those Tadpoles are almost done destroying your friends!
We were making an ANTIDOTE!!!
It's in this balloon!

All we have to do is Pop it...
...and those tadPoles will all Lose their SUPA Powers!!!!!
You better go hide in that swamp now, Molly...
...and stay under the water so ya won't breathe the antidote!
That way You won't Lose YOUR Supa Powers!!!
Okay! See ya Later!!!

AHA!
Hey!
You Guys are in BIG TROUBLE Now!
OH, FAIR FAIRY!
What do You WANT NOW???
Those two Kids were trying to trick You!
They Put ANTIDOTE GAS in this balloon!

If your tadpoles breathe it...
...they'll lose all of their superpowers!!!
Antidote gas, eh?
Yeah! And the only place that's safe is that swamp over there!!!
Is that so?
Yup!
Well that gives me a SPLENDID IDEA!

OK, TADPOLES– LISTEN UP!!!!
I want you all to hide in that SWAMP over there!
Stay underwater, and don't breathe the air for a few minutes!!!
OK, Mommy!
See ya Later!
Bye, Mom!

Now I'm Going to deal with YOU!
GRAB
You couldn't follow orders, could You?
You Just HAD to do Your own thing!
Well You're in Big Trouble now, Little girl!!!
WHAT ARE YOU GRINNIN' ABOUT?

Meanwhile...
PLIP PLIP PLIP PLIP PLIP
PLIP PLIP PLIP PLIP PLIP PLIP PLIP PLIP PLIP
PLIP PLIP PLIP PLIP PLIP PLIP PLIP PLIP PLIP PLIP PLIP PLIP
PLIP PLIP PLIP PLIP
POP
BLUB BLUB BLUB

Mean-While...
You'd better wipe that SMILE off of Your face, Young Lady...
...because things are about to Get SERIOUS!!!
He's Gonna Pop that balloon and...
...and...

KLUNK
W-What Happened???
LOOK!
chief

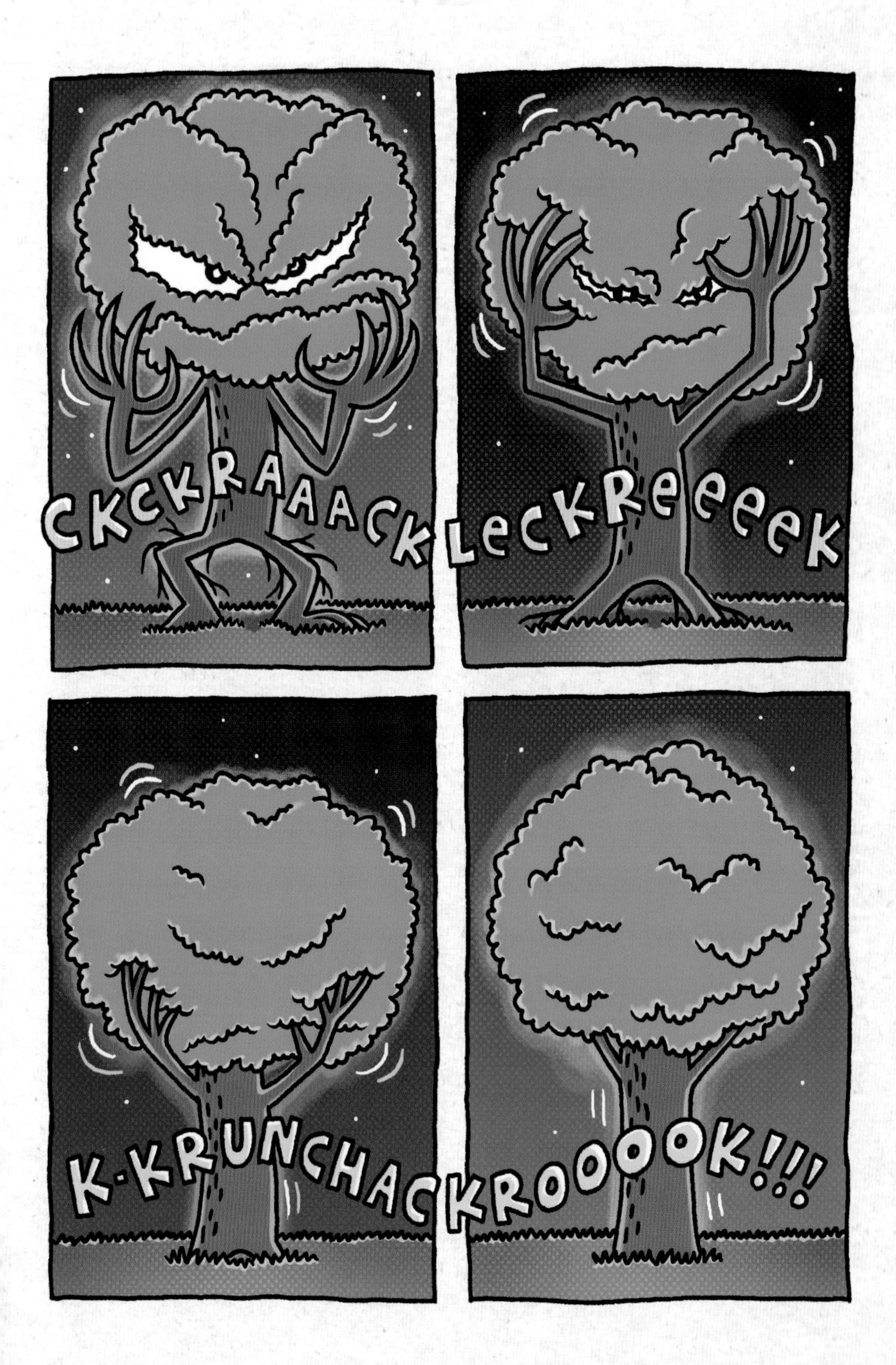
CKCKRAAACKLECKREEEEK
K-KRUNCHACKROOOOK!!!

THAT'S NOT FAIR!
THAT ANTIDOTE RUINED EVERYTHING!
Hey, wait a minute!
THere's No Antidote in this balloon, is there???
Nope.
YOU LIED to Me!!! YOU BETRAYED Me!!

I guess I did...
... GRAMPA!
Zuzu's the real hero Today!!!
She poured the antidote into the swamp and saved the world!!!
HOORAY FOR ZUZU!!!
Chief
whisper
whisper
whisper

Let's get out of here while we've Got a chance!!!
I'm with You!!!
But soon...
Puff Huff
Huff Puff
Huff Puff
Puff
Huff Huff
...and then...
Coco's Cupcakes
Yum!
OPEN 24 Hrs.
Heeave-Hooo
Heeave-Hooo
Heeave-Hooo
Heeave-Hoo
Heeave-Hooo
I can't walk much farther!
Yum!
HOT COFFEE
It's okay! I think we got away!!!
Really?

Lick
Lick
Lick
CK-CRACK
COCO'S CUPCAKES
Yeah! They're all still back there congratulating themselves!!!
Wow! We got SO LUCKY!
KRACK
Lick
Lick
COCO'S CUPCAKES
I know! We got away with no comeuppance whatsoever!!!
COCO'S CUPCAKES
We're the luckiest villains EVER!!!

CRASH!
Hey, Look! Commander Cupcake did it AGAin!
He captured the Fair fairy AND Grampa!!!
You two criminals are Going to JAiL!

NOT SO FAST!
This isn't Grampa! This is my Papa!
Sniff Sniff
But he looks Just Like Grampa!!!
Show 'em, 80-HD!!!

RiP
Rip
SOAPY WATER
No! WAit!!!
80-HD's BEAUTY SALON
iN FLiP-O-RAMA
Left hand here.

Gentle Rinse
Delicate cleanse
Relaxing Blow Dry
OFF ON
SUPA DRY 2000
Right Thumb here.

Gentle Rinse
Delicate cleanse
Relaxing Blow Dry
OFF ON
SUPA DRY 2000

TWANG
See?
BONK
Okay, I'm Convinced!
Works for me!
Let's Go, Grampa!
IT'S NOT FAIR!

Do Good, Flippy

Hey, what happened?
Did we miss anything?
No, not really.
Chief
Coco's Cupcakes
Costumes
The bad guys went to jail...
... and Commander Cupcake saved the day again!
He DID NOT!!!
HOORAY FOR COMMANDER CUPCAKE!!!
Chief
Coco's Cupcakes

Alright, let's Go, Kid!
Hey, Papa, Flippy and Molly don't have anywhere to Live.
Can they stay with us for a while?
Pleeease?
Please? Please?
Please?
Please?
Supa-Dupa Please?
Well, okay. But
YAY!

Bye-bye, everybody! Let's all play again tomorrow, okay?
chief
C'mon, Flippy! Let's Go!!!
Thanks, Guys... ...but I can't.
Why not?
I think I'm needed elsewhere.

Where, Flippy?
Well, there are twenty-one baby tadpoles in that swamp back there...
... and I'll bet they're feeling pretty lonely and afraid all by themselves.
I remember how that felt.
So I was thinking...

...maybe they could use a friend.
You were so Good to me when I was in fish JaiL, L.P.
You made comics for me every day!
You inspired me! You Kept me Going!
Now it's my turn to **DO GOOD!**
Hey! I wanna Do Good, too!!!

Well you can help me if ya want!
OKAY!
And you guys can visit us at the swamp anytime!!!
Yeah! You still have to teach me how to make comics!
I will!
Maybe you can teach all twenty-two of us!
OKAY!
Well, let's go, Kiddo!
BYe, Li'l Petey!
BYe, old guy!

And so...
See, Papa?
I TOLD Ya Flippy was a Good Guy!
Yeah. I guess so.
He's changing the world!
Well, I don't know about that!
I mean, come on!

All he's really doing is looking after a few baby tadpoles.
That's not really gonna change the world!
Maybe not...
...but it'll change their world!

Maybe You're right, Kid.
I am?
I was RIGHT about something?
I said MAYBE!
I WAS RIGHT About SOMETHING!

Sweeeet!
The

End

FORMER FISH FELON FINDS FAMILY

Flippy the bionic psychokinetic butterfly fish was released from fish jail last week, and is already making an impact in our community. In this exclusive interview, Flippy shares his inspiring story:

Q. How has life changed since you were in Fish Jail?
A. WELL, I MOVED INTO A SWAMP AND NOW I'M RAISING A BUNCH OF BABY TADPOLES.
Q. How did you meet them?
A. WE MET LAST WEEK WHEN THEY TRIED TO DESTROY THE PLANET.
Q. Weren't you afraid of them?
A. NAH. I KNEW THEY WERE GOOD KIDS DEEP DOWN INSIDE. AND I WAS RIGHT.

Q. Were they happy to see you?
A. THEY DIDN'T RECOGNIZE ME. THEY HAD NO MEMORY OF THEIR TERRIFYING ORDEAL. IN FACT, THEY ALL STARTED CALLING ME "DADDY."

●●●●○UP&P LTE
11:03 AM
pilkey.com
91%
Menu
Q. So what did you do?
A. I HAD NO CHOICE. I ADOPTED THEM ALL.
Q. So what's next for you and your new family?
A. RIGHT NOW I'M TEACHING EVERYBODY TO READ AND WRITE. MY FRIEND MOLLY IS HELPING, AND CAT KID IS TEACHING US ALL HOW TO MAKE OUR OWN COMICS!
CAT KID'S COMIC CLUB!
Local kitten Li'l Petey has started his own comic club, and it's gaining new members every day. If you would like to start your OWN chapter of Cat Kid's Comic Club, go to scholastic.com/catkidclub to download everything you need. It's free and it's FUN!
DOG MAN IS GO!
An ALL-NEW Dog Man novel is coming SOON, and it's going to be the BEST ONE YET!!! The title of the all-

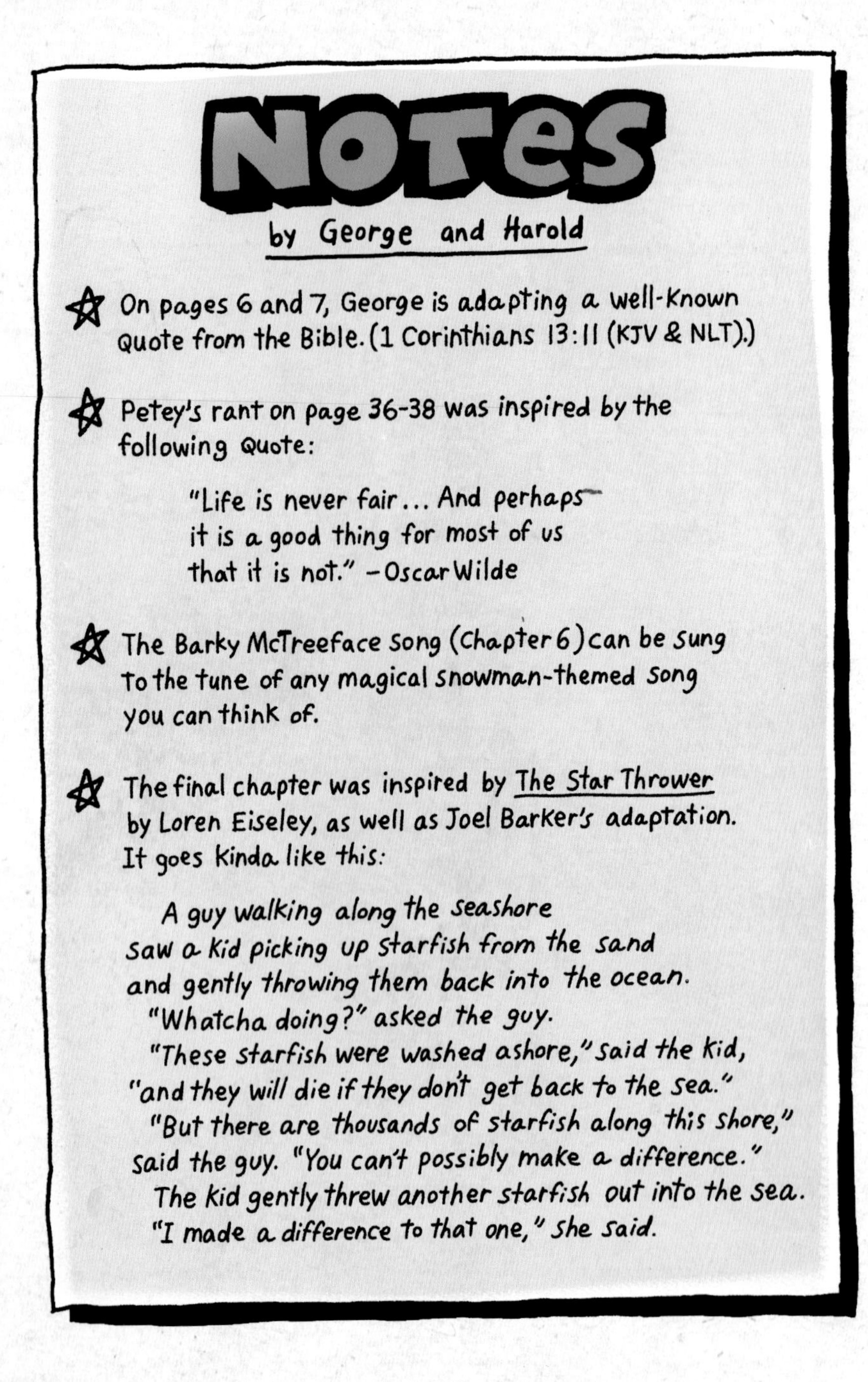

NOTES

by George and Harold

- On pages 6 and 7, George is adapting a well-Known Quote from the Bible. (1 Corinthians 13:11 (KJV & NLT).)

- Petey's rant on page 36-38 was inspired by the following Quote:

  "Life is never fair... And perhaps it is a good thing for most of us that it is not." –Oscar Wilde

- The Barky McTreeface Song (Chapter 6) can be sung to the tune of any magical snowman-themed song you can think of.

- The final chapter was inspired by The Star Thrower by Loren Eiseley, as well as Joel Barker's adaptation. It goes Kinda like this:

  A guy walking along the seashore saw a kid picking up starfish from the sand and gently throwing them back into the ocean.
  "Whatcha doing?" asked the guy.
  "These starfish were washed ashore," said the kid, "and they will die if they don't get back to the sea."
  "But there are thousands of starfish along this shore," said the guy. "You can't possibly make a difference."
  The kid gently threw another starfish out into the sea.
  "I made a difference to that one," she said.

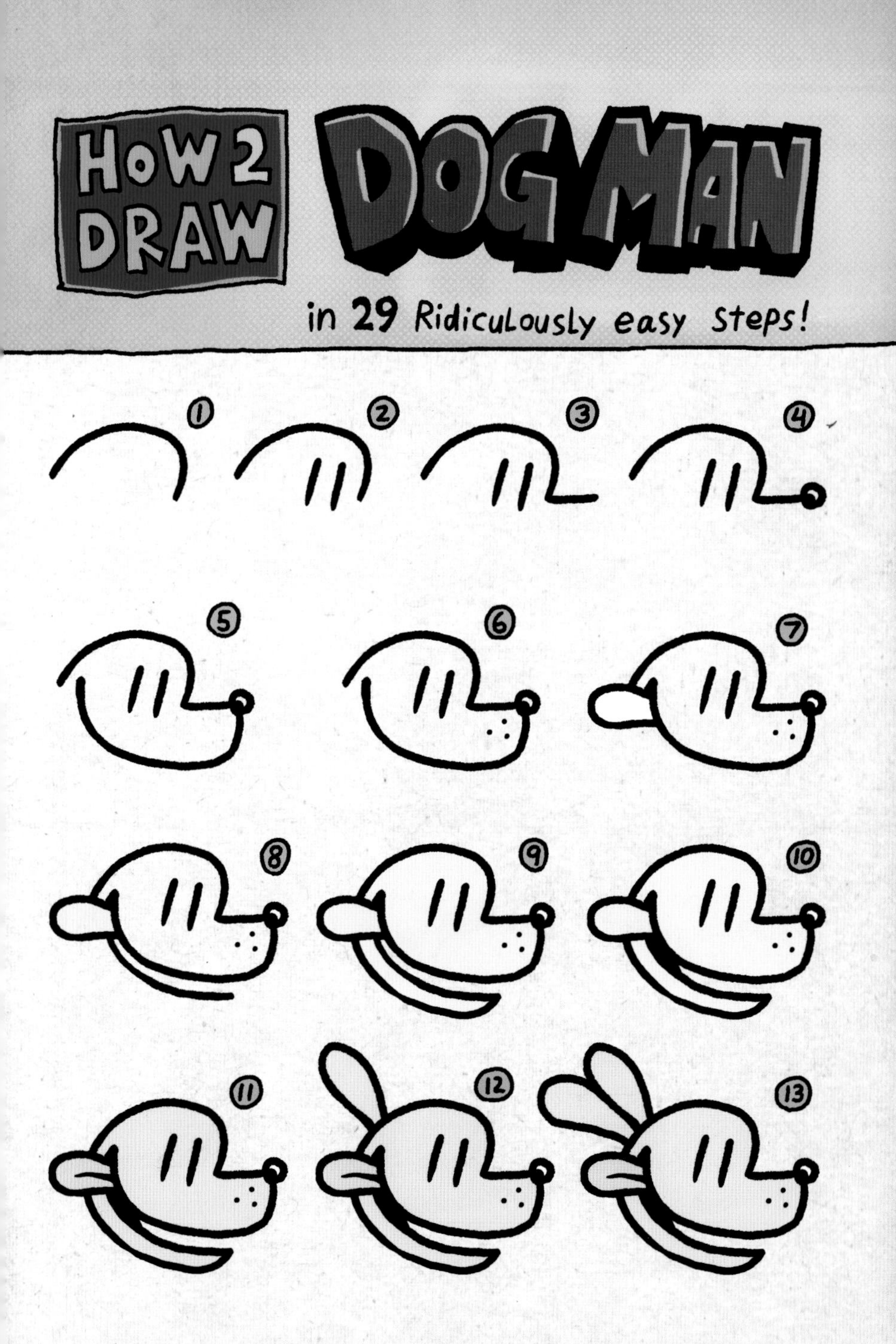
HOW 2 DRAW
DOG MAN
in 29 Ridiculously easy steps!
1
2
3
4
5
6
7
8
9
10
11
12
13

14
15
16
17

18
19
20

21
22
23

24
25
26

27
28
29

HOW 2 DRAW
Li'L Petey
in 21 Ridiculously Easy steps!
1
2
3
4
5
6
7
8
9
10
11
12
13
14
15
16
17
18

19
20
21
HOW 2 DRAW
MOLLY
in 9 Ridiculously Easy Steps!
1
2
3
4
5
6
7
8
9

HOW 2 DRAW
ZUZU
in 17 Ridiculously easy steps!
1
2
3
4
5
6
7
8
9
10
11
12
13
14
15
16
17

HOW 2 DRAW
McBARKY TREEFACE
in 24 Ridiculously Easy Steps!
2
3
4

1

5

6

7

8

9

10

11

12

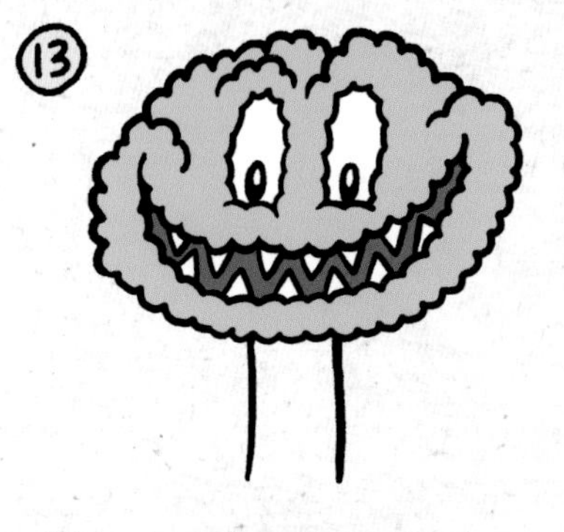
13

14

15

16

17

18

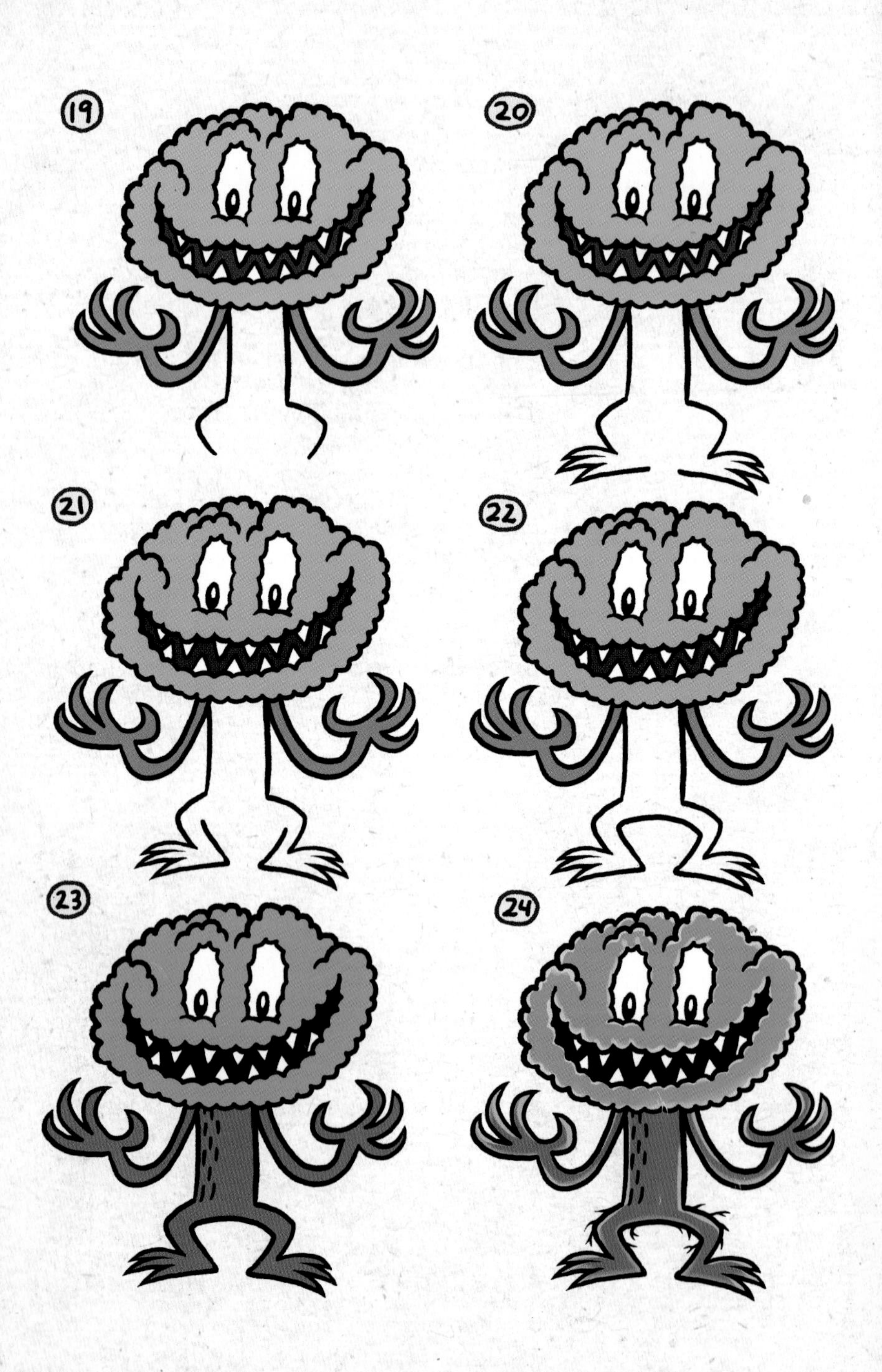
19
20
21
22
23
24

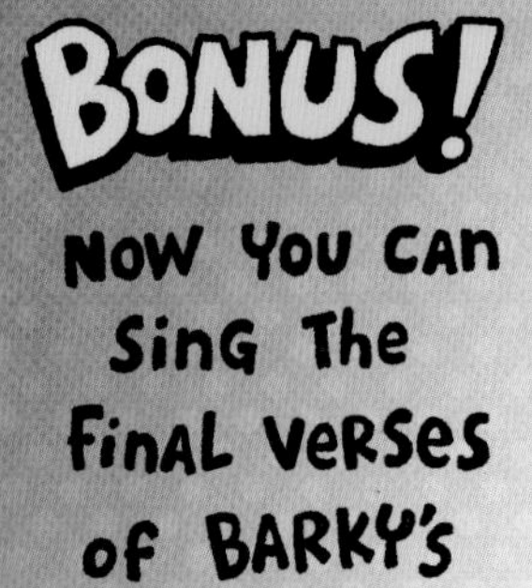

Oh, Barky McTreeface
Knew the moon was bright that night.
So he grabbed his foes with his hands and toes
And he squeezed them really tight!

Then all the tadpoles
flew into a swampy bay.
And the medicine Zuzu poured right in
Made their powers go away!

So Barky dropped our heroes
and he turned back to a tree.
Then the bad guys went to jail and
that's the end of our story.

Now Barky McTreeface
is so peaceful, calm, and zen.
And if you do good like ya know you should
then he won't come back again!!!

Peace-ity peace-peace, zen-ity zen
Look at Barky now!
Do-ity Do-Do, Good-ity Good
He won't come back no-how!!!

YOU BETTER NOT!

OLD LADY JAIL

GET READING W
The Adventures of CAPTAIN UNDERPANTS FULL COLOR
Action
Thrills
Laffs
THE FIRST EPIC NOVEL BY
DAV PILKEY
CALDECOTT HONOR ARTIST
FULL COLOR CAPTAIN UNDERPANTS AND THE ATTACK OF THE TALKING TOILETS
More Action
More Laffs
More Flip-O-Rama
THE SECOND EPIC NOVEL BY
DAV PILKEY
CALDECOTT HONOR ARTIST
FULL COLOR CAPTAIN UNDERPANTS AND THE INVASION OF THE INCREDIBLY NAUGHTY CAFETERIA LADIES FROM OUTER SPACE (and the Subsequent Assault of the Equally Evil Lunchroom Zombie Nerds)
Tons O' Fun
Lots O' Laffs
Flip-O-Rama
THE THIRD EPIC NOVEL BY
DAV PILKEY
CALDECOTT HONOR ARTIST
FULL COLOR CAPTAIN UNDERPANTS AND THE PERILOUS PLOT OF PROFESSOR POOPYPANTS
THE FOURTH EPIC NOVEL BY
DAV PILKEY
CALDECOTT HONOR ARTIST
FULL COLOR CAPTAIN UNDERPANTS AND THE WRATH OF THE WICKED WEDGIE WOMAN
THE FIFTH EPIC NOVEL BY
DAV PILKEY
CALDECOTT HONOR ARTIST
FULL COLOR CAPTAIN UNDERPANTS AND THE BIG, BAD BATTLE OF THE BIONIC BOOGER BOY PART 1: THE NIGHT OF THE NASTY NOSTRIL NUGGETS
THE SIXTH EPIC NOVEL BY
DAV PILKEY
CALDECOTT HONOR ARTIST
FULL COLOR CAPTAIN UNDERPANTS AND THE BIG, BAD BATTLE OF THE BIONIC BOOGER BOY PART 2: THE REVENGE OF THE RIDICULOUS ROBO-BOOGERS
THE SEVENTH EPIC NOVEL BY
DAV PILKEY
CALDECOTT HONOR ARTIST
FULL COLOR CAPTAIN UNDERPANTS AND THE PREPOSTEROUS PLIGHT OF THE PURPLE POTTY PEOPLE
THE EIGHTH EPIC NOVEL BY
DAV PILKEY
CALDECOTT HONOR ARTIST
FULL COLOR CAPTAIN UNDERPANTS AND THE TERRIFYING RE-TURN OF TIPPY TINKLETROUSERS
THE NINTH EPIC NOVEL BY
DAV PILKEY
CALDECOTT HONOR ARTIST
Download the free Planet Pilkey app to start your digital adventure! Create an avatar, make your own comics, and more at planetpilkey.com!
PLANET PILKEY
Download on the App Store
GET IT ON Google Play
PLANET PILKEY
SCHOLASTIC

TH DAV PILKEY!

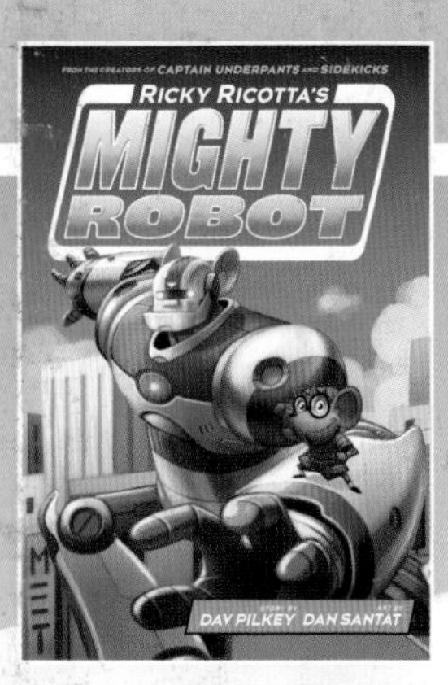

"A fun introduction to chapter books."
— SCHOOL LIBRARY JOURNAL

ABOUT THE AUTHOR-ILLUSTRATOR

When Dav Pilkey was a kid, he was diagnosed with ADHD and dyslexia. Dav was so disruptive in class that his teachers made him sit out in the hall every day. Luckily, Dav loved to draw and make up stories. He spent his time in the hallway creating his own original comic books.

In the second grade, Dav Pilkey made a comic book about a superhero named Captain Underpants. Since then, he has been creating books that explore fun, positive themes and inspire readers everywhere.

ABOUT THE COLORIST

Jose Garibaldi grew up on the South Side of Chicago. As a kid, he was a daydreamer and a doodler, and now it's his full-time job to do both. Jose is a professional illustrator, painter, and cartoonist who has created work for many organizations, including Nickelodeon, MAD Magazine, Cartoon Network, Disney, and THE EPIC ADVENTURES OF CAPTAIN UNDERPANTS for DreamWorks Animation. He lives in Los Angeles, California, with his wonder dogs, Herman and Spanky.